BILLY LE ABOUT ANXIETY

WRITTEN BY
DOROTA PERKINS

ILLUSTRATIONS
ANDREA POLLARD

2 COLOURING
BONUS
PAGES INSIDE

BILLY LEARNS ABOUT ANXIETY
COPYRIGHT © DOROTA PERKINS, 2022

FIRST EDITION: MARCH 2022

AUTHOR
DOROTA PERKINS

ILLUSTRATOR
ANDREA POLLARD

COPY EDITOR
CAITLIN OWEN

CONTENT EDITOR
LAURA CAPUTO-WICKHAM

DESIGN AND LAYOUT
DOROTA PERKINS

ISBN (PAPERBACK):978-1-7398472-3-4

AUTHOR`S WEBSITE
WWW.DOROTAPERKINS.COM

This book belongs to:

_____

"Here, little Stormy," sings Billy,
giving his pet lizard a little rub.

But, suddenly "Aa... Aa... Aa..."

"ARRGGGHHHH!" shrieks Billy, and with a SNAP, Stormy bites him on his thumb.

"Ouch!" says Billy, running to his mum.

"Why did Stormy bite me?" Billy cries, rubbing his sore thumb.

"She was just scared," replies Mummy. "She thought you wanted to hurt her."

"Hurt her?!" asks Billy. "But I'd never do that!"
"She didn't know," says Mummy.

"You see, when Stormy is scared, she'll do one
of three things."

FREEZE

FLIGHT
(RUN)

FIGHT

"And this time, she chose to fight."

"Did you know, Billy, that we all have lizard brains? Me, you, Daddy."

"Even Nana?"

"Yes," smiles Mummy, "even Nana. We all share Stormy's flight or fight instinct when things feel a little... too much."

Mummy puts a plaster on Billy's thumb.
"All better now," she says.

After learning about fight, and flight,
Billy goes to tidy up his bedroom.

Whilst putting the toys away, he sees a
spider behind the toy box...

"MUMMY! There is a big spider in my bedroom!" Billy screams.

He feels his heart pounding, his face turning red, and his hands shaking.

He runs away from his bedroom as fast as he can!

"That spider was huge! Bigger than any spider I have ever seen! " Billy shouts.

Then suddenly, Billy stops.

He looks at his Mummy
and mutters, "I think I've just
pulled a Stormy!"

"

"Maybe you have."

"But Mummy," he asks, "why don't you, Daddy, or Nana ever pull a Stormy?" "We do sometimes," replies Mummy.

"It's normal to get a bit scared, worried, anxious...

But we also have a superpower.
It's called the NEOCORTEX."

"The neocortex is an extra brain that helps
us to think, plan, prepare, and control our
emotions."

"I want to learn to use my neocortex too!" says Billy.

"But how do I do that?"

SUPER POWER?

"Well," says Mummy, "our strongest feelings, and emotions last for just a few minutes. During that time there are different things you could do."

"You could try splashing cold water on your hot face."

"You could say a mantra. A sentence that you repeat over and over again until the strongest feeling of worry goes away.

What would your mantra be, Billy?" asks Mummy

"Hmmm... how about, 'it will all get better'?"

"IT WILL ALL GET BETTER"

"We need to accept our lizard brains. But it's also good to know that we can keep our instincts under control," says Mummy.

"I like the idea of being a little like Stormy," smiles Billy.

"She's the best pet lizard in the world! But I also like that I can control my emotions."

With a smile, Billy gives Stormy a little rub, making sure to be super...

Extra...

Extremely...

Gentle.

THE END

COLOURING PAGE 1

COLOURING PAGE 2

Dear Reader!

Thank you for purchasing my book!
Your feedback via Amazon reviews motivates me to write more books for children. Please share your views!

If you would like to receive printable calming strategies, and feelings flashcards please go to www.dorotaperkins.com and leave your e-mail.

If you liked this book you might also like one of my recent books "Mindful of my feelings."

Best Regards
Dorota Perkins

Printed in Great Britain
by Amazon